FREE AT LAST

BY

MRS. JANE S. COLLINS

The Black Heritage Library Collection

BOOKS FOR LIBRARIES PRESS

FREEPORT, NEW YORK

1972

First Published 1896
Reprinted 1972

Reprinted from a copy in the
Fisk University Library Negro Collection

INTERNATIONAL STANDARD BOOK NUMBER:
0-8369-8962-7

LIBRARY OF CONGRESS CATALOG CARD NUMBER:
71-37586

PRINTED IN THE UNITED STATES OF AMERICA
BY
NEW WORLD BOOK MANUFACTURING CO., INC.
HALLANDALE, FLORIDA 33009

FREE AT LAST

❧

By MRS. JANE S. COLLINS

Author of "Emma's Triumph" and other Stories,
Etc., Etc.

❧

PITTSBURGH:
PRESS OF MURDOCH, KERR & CO., INCORPORATED,
53 AND 55 NINTH STREET,
1896

J.C. Beard, Pinx.

FREE AT LAST

To the
noble Mother of a
brave son, who gave his life that the slave
might be free, this book is
affectionately dedicated by the Author.

AUTHOR'S PREFACE.

IN presenting this book to the public, no apology is offered for selecting, as my themes, subjects that have been used over and over again. The slave problem is settled, but the drink is still an unsolved question before the American people.

My interest in the colored people dates from early childhood, at the family altar, where the Father of Mercies was daily asked, "That the yoke might be broken, and the oppressed go free."

In the *National Era* I read to my father the stirring speeches of Congressmen, and I heard the subject of slavery discussed in the pulpit and on the platform. At the opening of the war I saw the gathering forces on the border land; heard the cry, "To arms"; visited the sick in the hospital; made shirts and scraped lint for the wounded. I rejoice that my father's family would not accept of slaves left them, but set them free.

To-day, the stars and stripes float over "this land of the free and home of the brave" more united than ever, through suffering.

Scarcely had this war-cloud passed over when the gathering forces of women, as well as men, engaged in a mighty conflict with a more terrible foe. Mothers and sisters kneeled on curb-stones, pleading for protection to their boys from the saloon. The eloquent Gough, and gentle women pleaded in their behalf.

The cry comes from the millions of Anglo-Africans at our doors, in the South land, "Come over and help us." Shall they be evangelized and raised to a higher plane of civilization?

To assist in this work, is the design of this little book.

J. S. C.

CONTENTS.

ILLUSTRATIONS.

CHAPTER I.

THE NEW LIFE.

"Thine eye hath seen the bondsman's tear;
Thine ear hath heard the bondsman's prayer."
— *Whittier.*

"Ise berry happy dis ebenin"; said Sam, with a broad grin on his face.

"What makes yo' so happy?"

Sam paused a moment, and sitting down in his chair, said: "Yo' see, Percy, Ise a free man. I calls no man massa now. I kin cum an' go as I please. Aint dat enuff?

"I reckon it is, Sam ; I likes dat, too, but I don't likes hevin nuffin ; to be poah. I tho't dat freedom meant a piece of lan', an' flouah in de bar'l, an' a heap ob bacon; but dis chile haint seed none of it yit."

"It is mighty hard to be sot down widout a picayune in yo' pocket, an' no massa ter look ter ter 'sply de chickens. 'Spose we'll hev ter scratch fur ourselves now."

"I 'spose. I've allus worked hard an' kin do it agin; but I likes ter hev suthin' fur my work, don't yo'?"

"Laws yes, an' plenty ob it, too."

These men were among the poorest of the freedmen at Nashville, Tenn. Like many others, they thought the Government had land for them, and when they did not get it, were disappointed. They did not realize that the Government had a big contract on hand, and that it would take time to adjust matters.

The freedom of four millions of slaves, and the preservation of the Union, were achievements not to be despised. How the freedmen would live, was an after-thought. War was the Nation's cruel way of throwing off the yoke which bound these human beings in slavery.

It took money as well as time and lives to carry on the war which freed them. For centuries the prayers and tears of this poor, oppressed people had gone up before the Lord, and he heard them. No longer were they to be bought and sold, as cattle and horses in the stalls. They were free to think and act for themselves ; but freedom brought poverty and great suffering.

Hardly had Mr. Lincoln issued the proclamation when thousands of those

poor creatures left the places they
called home, some to find transporta-
tion by the army to a safe retreat,
others to join the ranks of soldiers, to
help free themselves. Many crowded
the cities, hoping to find something to do.

The United States Government furnished some rations ; but with it all,
there was great destitution among
them. Many died from starvation.
Everything was in a chaotic state ;
both armies left ruin in their path.

During General Thomas' occupancy
of Nashville many found shelter there.
They erected small shanties, with. sel-
dom anything but the earth for floors,
in the center of which they drove stakes
and hung cross-bars of iron for the ket-
tles, in which they cooked their meals.
A dozen would crowd into a small

room, where all ate and slept. A little straw in a corner of the room, and an army blanket served for a bed for all the family. This description is given, that the reader may have some idea of their extreme destitution.

Many were very ignorant, having been neglected by those who should have taken an interest in them. But ignorant as they were of books, they knew what freedom meant. At night they gathered in their miserable quarters and sang their plantation songs, which often inspired them with hope in the future, and they were happy.

Every day brought new recruits. Loved ones long separated, in time found each other; then there was rejoicing, and the scanty fare was shared in common.

Among the children were many
bright, intelligent ones, whose great
need was something to educate and ele-
vate, and make them useful men and
women.   To reach these with Chris-
tianizing influences, the Church imme-
diately set to work.

The Government could not long continue to help them, or enter into any
great scheme to ameliorate their condition.   The vast expense of the war
made this impossible. It would take
time and means to accomplish a change
among them. Something would have
to be done to improve them morally
and socially. This was needed for self-
protection, if for no other reason.
Their habits were bad ; many were lazy
and shiftless, and needed to be taught.
Long accustomed to lean on others,

they had not learned lessons of self-reliance and self-help. If to-day they had "hoe cake and bacon," they were satisfied; they had no thought for the future. Kind people, North, whose prayers for years had been for "liberty to the captives," were ready and waiting to help them. Teachers were sent to instruct them in temporal and spiritual things. The American Missionary Association, founded in 1846, anticipating the need, opened Sabbath and day schools among them; cabins and the deserted mansions being used for this purpose.

Thus early some were taught the way of life, and the occupations necessary to their elevation and future usefulness. Of the church organizations, the United Presbyterian has the honor of being among, if not the very first, to send teachers to the freedmen. In 1862-3 they opened schools at Goodrich Landing, Miss., and Nashville, Tenn. Young men and women of culture, with the true missionary spirit and devotion, left pleasant homes to go to the South and labor in this most noble work. Through their persevering efforts great good was accomplished.

A pioneer teacher, Rev. Joseph G. McKee, whose life was sacrificed in his effort to improve the condition of the freedmen, suffered many privations. He organized the work when it was very unpopular. People pointed the finger of scorn at him on the streets. Often he had not where to lay his head, being compelled to sleep under army wagons, in stable lofts, in the rough

REV. JOSEPH G. McKEE,

BORN NOVEMBER 10TH, 1832, AT ANAHILT, COUNTY DOWN, IRELAND.

cabins of these poor people, or wherever he could find a resting place.
Once he found forty-two persons in one
small room, without a chimney, cooking
their meals on stones and bricks in the
center of the floor. Among them were
sick women and poor, weakly children,
without food, or fire to cook their meals,
or keep them warm. He often cut
"wood, carried it on his back in par-
cels, and distributed it to the suffering." The untold hardships he en-
dured among the thousands of "contra-
bands," who came to Nashville for shelter, will never be known. With the
temperature at six degrees below zero
and wood at $40 a cord, there was
great suffering.

This faithful friend of the slave never
faltered, though the difficulties he en-

countered would have crushed many. Without a murmur or a complaint he calmly trusted his cause to the God whom he served, and who gave him grace to bear all his trials. But the exposure was too much for him ; he contracted a cold which brought on repeated hemorrhages, causing great weakness. As he went about ministering to the wants of the freedmen, they said of him, " Massa 'Kee is an angel jis cum down frum Heben, to help us in our time of need." He was a cheerful, happy man, kind alike to friends and foes ; and when forced to lay down this grand work, so dear to his heart, thousands mourned.

Mr. McKee believed a bright future awaited the colored race, and to this end inaugurated reforms in the schools.

Being a member of the City Council he secured the passage of a law requiring the City Board of Education to assume the supervision of six schools, taught in what was called the McKee school building in Nashville.   His teachers, who passed examination, were paid the same as teachers in the other public schools of the city.*

It was a great satisfaction to see the local laws so changed that a man or woman could teach a negro, without being fined fifty dollars in the courts, or being threatened with hanging by the mob.

He began to realize his ideal when he gathered a room full of boys and girls into a Normal Class for instruction, and opened a training school for girls and

*Diary.

women to be taught knitting and sew-
ing. "He won for this work the support of the city."

He gave five years of faithful service
to this worthy work for the Master.
When he died the cause of temperance,
social purity and education generally,
lost an able champion. But his works
follow him. Many now rise up and call
him blessed.

When he left his father's house in Ireland, a lone boy of sixteen, to come to
America, his friends wondered. Though
he knew not its nature, he had a mission
of great good to poor, oppressed humanity. He longed to do something to
lift up the degraded from darkness and
sensuality to light, purity and usefulness. His mission included the salvation
of men from the drink slavery which

threatened them. His first school was opened in September, 1863. He afterward occupied a building called the McKee School, erected by the churches, near the now famous Fiske University, named in honor of its founder, Clinton B. Fiske. Church and Sabbath school services were held every Lord's day. Old and young were taught to read and study the Bible. Gray-haired men and women wept with joy when first they read the name of "Jesus," "Master," etc. At last the long-looked-for day had come when they could read God's own book, and they were happy.

One* who labored for a time with Mr. McKee, says : "Another work, but closely akin to that for the freedmen, was for the prisoners in the penitentiary.

---

*Rev. S. Collins, D. D.

Probably three-fourths of six or seven
hundred there were colored men, ex
slaves, against whom there was an im-
placable prejudice. They, and too often
their white friends, on the slightest pre-
text, were consigned to hard labor and to
the cruelties of heartless prison-labor-
contractors. This gratified both the race
prejudice among the whites, and the love
of money on the part of the contractors,
who made fortunes out of convict labor.
Mr. McKee seeing and pitying these
poor unfortunates, with the consent of
the more humane prison warden, in
1868 organized in the penitentiary a
Sabbath school, in which some two or
three hundred convicts readily took
part. Some very efficient teachers were
secured from among them. Souls were
there "born again" and trained for
Christ and for glory. From this has

largely grown the more efficient moral training now generally prevalent in the larger prisons and reformatories of our own and other Protestant countries.

" Another step taken by Mr. McKee in the prison work, was the organization of a prayer-meeting among the convicts —the only one of the kind we have ever known. The proposition (made by a friend, March, 1868,) at first appeared visionary and impracticable ; but it was tried. The poor prisoners at first shrank from it. But some there had taken Christ's yoke upon them—a few before, but more since coming within those walls, and these agreed to and did take part in the devotions of that prayer-meeting. For years it was well attended and bore fruit. At one time it was said that not less than a hundred

3

and fifty different persons would lead in
prayer whenever called upon, a grand
testimonial to the Christian faithfulness
of that humble, most diligent and devoted servant of God, Rev. Jos. G. Mc-
Kee.   He was small in stature and
feeble in body ; but strong in faith he
overcame the world, and now wears a
crown of victory with many gems, to the
glory of the Lord Jesus."

Thousands gathered into the schools,
their ages ranging from 5 to 50, all eager
and thankful to learn.   Those otherwise
employed during the day, attended the
night schools, some walking several
miles to do this.   Their homespun clothing, never very good, was often so worn
and torn that it could no longer be
patched.   Kind friends North, who sent
them teachers, also sent boxes of new

and second-hand clothing by the ton, to be distributed among them. All able to earn a little were required to pay a nominal price for good suits, thus teaching them habits of honesty and independence. At the same time it furnished a fund with which other clothing and material, not supplied in boxes, could be procured.

The kind men and women, whose love to do good led them to leave friends and home to labor among them, received but little sympathy from the whites around them. There was odium connected with teaching the freedmen. Many of the freedmen themselves looked with suspicion on those who went to teach them. Nor were the sufferings and privations of teachers realized or rewarded as they should have been.

Still they went in and out of the rude cabins of their scholars, carrying aid and cheer to the living, and ministering spiritual comfort to the sick and dying. Women, often the greatest sufferers, were taught to accept their lot, and cheered with the hope that a better day was coming.

A marked change was soon visible among them. Adults and children improved every way. The education given was practical, not head culture only, but heart and hand as well. They were taught to reverence and obey God as supreme, and next their parents and teachers.

CHAPTER II.

IMPROVING OPPORTUNITIES.

In one of the schools for the freedmen our hero, as will be seen from the sequel, began his life work.

George was an unusually bright boy, black as black could be, contradicting the idea so often advanced that intelligence could not be found in the pure African. He was the eldest of six children. His father, whose health was poor, could not earn enough to feed so many, hence the mother took in washing. Her great ambition was to give her children an education. When the schools were opened she sent George, who, though his clothes were patched, always was neat and clean. His was an honest face, that carried sunshine wherever he went. He made such rapid progress in school that he was not long in mastering the first lessons in arithmetic and other studies. His books, though somewhat worse for the wear, having done good service in schools North before he received them, were well cared for. His teacher was proud of him, and before the end of the year set him to hear some of the classes.

His mother's name was Abigail, which signifies, "joy of her father," but for convenience she was called Abby. Like her namesake, she had a mission. She was one of those irrepressible women who always pray and speak in meeting.

This she conscientiously did, even in the presence of her superiors in learning. Her place was never vacant in prayer-meeting, and often the Spirit moved her to speak when others wanted to. She was a good woman, whose honesty and sincerity no one ever doubted. If George grew up 'spected like young massa, she would be happy.

George was an active boy, and was always in demand, because he could be trusted. He did his work promptly, without a murmur, though it was a trial to be kept from school. His father had been a plantation hand, and in his youth possessed great muscular strength ; but over-work had brought on some nervous disease, which disabled him for manual labor. This made it hard on his wife,

who was an industrious, careful house-
keeper. Their crowded room afforded
but few facilities for George to study.
They were too poor to have the luxury
of a candle, but he had the privilege of
gathering bits of boards and pine knots
in a neighboring shop. These he
stored away to use for light.

Like many a white boy, he began
his education under great difficulties.
Kind people North, ever on the alert
for the comfort and improvement of
the freedmen, continued to send clothing, books and other useful articles,
which added much to their comfort and
appearance. Men's and women's suits,
but little worn, were sent in quantities
from Pittsburgh, Boston, Philadelphia
and other places all over the North,
which, when altered, made suits for old

and young. Many a young man got his first suit of broadcloth out of boxes sent from the North. On Sabbath, when they assembled for service in the mission, dressed in good clothes, they looked respectable, and began to act like gentlemen.

There was much to be done in removing their superstitions in regard to signs and omens before they would be intelligent Christians. The " traditions of the fathers," handed down from time immemorial, were religiously observed. A century of education would be necessary to their removal.

The fourth year of freedom found the schools in a more flourishing condition. The mission buildings were increasing in number and size. Thousands now availed themselves of the privilege of attending school. This was a golden opportunity for the Christian Church to do more than it did, to save the freedmen from the Roman Catholic Church. There will be a sad reckoning for this neglect, in suffering them to lapse through Romanism into all the idolatries of the land from whence they came. "Inasmuch as ye did it not to one of these, ye did it not to me."

The door is still open, inviting all to work. It promises as rich rewards as ever it did. The freedmen are willing, nay anxious, to be instructed.

CHAPTER III.

With the dawn of freedom came a new temptation to the freedmen. They no sooner found they were their own masters than something else claimed the mastership. The drink demon, prevalent in slavery times, still troubled them.

"Just a little while, my son. It is too bad yer father got hisself inter trouble with dat dirty licker. Ef I hed de chance I'd turn ebry drop ob it into de ribbah."

"If I stay home from school, mother, I'll get behind with my lessons," said George, crying.

"Never mind, George, it won't be long. Stay at home and earn a little while your father ain't workin'."

"We had a good time befoah father got to drinkin'. We looked like white folks, with our nice table an' plenty ter eat, and kindling for light."

"'Deed we had, son; 'en we wuz happy; but I'se hearn dat when 'whiskey is in, wit is out.' Reckon yer father will drink, en we will have to bar it, hard as it is."

"I'm glad father did not kill anybody," said George, drawing a long sigh.

"Oh, dat would be a mighty sight harder," said his mother, her eyes filling with tears at the thought of such a terrible thing.

"Don't trouble yoself, mammy; I

will be a good son, and take care of yo'
all yo' days."

"God bress de chile. I'se sure yo'
will, my son. De good book says,
'H'ar now, my son, an' be wise ; don'
go wid wine tipplers.' Yo' father was
not wise, an' yer see what he cum ter."

"If he had kept out of Bill Holly's
company he would not be in prison
to-day," said George, very wisely.

"Dat's so," said his mother, with a
sigh.

Many learned to drink from their
masters' example. No matter how
poor they were, their masters encouraged them to save money for whiskey
on Christmas. Among those who had
fallen into drinking habits was George's
father. His physician prescribed liquor
for some disease, and he had become

4

so much addicted to its use, that he could not do without it.

Those who indulged were becoming idle, vicious and unreliable. Loafing prevailed in the neighborhood of the drinking places. Freedmen, as well as whites, were guilty of offenses for which they were sent to the penitentiary at Nashville, Tenn. On any day the chain-gang could be seen marching to and from the work in a stone quarry. Many of these were colored.

Not unfrequently colored men suffered for crimes committed by whites— men whose innocence could be proven beyond a doubt ; but because of their idle habits and their color, the blame rested on them.

The good missionary found George's father in the penitentiary. He could not tell how he came to be there. All he remembered was that he had been drinking, and was in court receiving his sentence for theft.

"I'se suah I nebbah took nuthin. Please get me outen dis place."

His case excited the sympathy of the good missionary, but he was powerless before the inexorable law. The prayer-meeting and Sabbath school inaugurated in the prison, proved a great blessing to the prisoners. This reform in prison work has been adopted with good results in other prisons North and South.

It could not be expected that an ignorant people would all do right. The wounds which generations of slavery made were too deep to be healed in one life time. Often when

parents were tempted and tried, their
spirits revived at seeing their children
growing up in intelligence under their
faithful teachers. This was compen-
sation enough for all the poverty and
hardships of their lot. The faith, which
was their solace for over two hundred
and fifty years, did not now forsake
them. They had prayed and believed
freedom would come; but the trials and
temptations were not thought of.

George had a manly pride which
made him feel very keenly his father's
imprisonment. He was never guilty
of dishonest tricks, such as often occur
among boys in school. He was too
well brought up by his teacher and
mother, whose home training made her
careful of her children. He was strong
and healthy, and could make a hand

now at any ordinary employment. He
rose bright and early to find something
to do. His straightforward look in a
man's eye, when asking for work, procured a job, with the promise that if
satisfactory, he should have another
when that was done. When he received his first money he hurried home,
and laying it in his mother's lap, said :

"Here, mammy, is my wages ; get
something for father with some of it."

The boys tried to tempt him to treat
to "'backer," but he told them he did
not use his money for such things.

Poor as the freedmen were, most of
them used tobacco. Brought up to
raise and handle it, they learned to like
it, if for nothing else than for the little
stimulus it gave, making them forget
their poverty, and for the time they

were happy. Women, as well as men, would sit for hours smoking their cob pipes. No matter if the meal in the barrel was low and they had nothing in the house, Topsy would spend her last dime for a pipe or a tin rabbit, or other useless thing.

George's mother had been a house servant, and was trained to care for the little things. While others were in need, she always had something laid up for a rainy day. She was comforted in having such a thoughtful son, whose acts of kindness helped to lighten her burdens.

George wanted to see his father, but the thought that he would have to go to the prison to see him was very humiliating.

"What is I heah foah? I'se dun

nuffin dat's wrong as I know ob," said
his father, weeping bitterly.

" That may be, father, but I can't get
you out of prison. Won't you promise
that you will never drink anymore ?"

" 'Deed I will. I'se berry sorry I has
dis bad habit. It is mighty trouble-
some. I'se allus hed sich mis'able
health, an' ole massa said: ' Why
don't yer try ole rye ?' an' I did, an' it
got de better ob me. Yer see, son, it
ain't safe fer medicine, no how."

" My teacher read in the good book,
' Wine is a mocker, strong drink is
raging; whosoever is deceived thereby
is not wise.'"

" Dat's de Bible doctrine, an' true as
preachin'. I'se sure yer won't drink,
son."

" 'Deed I will not. I want an educa-

tion, and to be respected like Colonel
G——."

Young as he was, when freed he
remembered white men whom he was
taught to respect as but little inferior to
his Maker. In his ignorance he imagined he would be like them. He had
not learned that some of those very
men had the same failing his father
had; that neither education nor color
in itself was a safeguard against temptation.

Tears stole down their cheeks when
they parted. Centuries of bondage
and ignorance could not entirely remove the finer feelings and affections
from the African heart. Their trials
rather intensified their love and interest
in one another. There was always
room in their homes, however poor,

for the aged and homeless man or woman, or for a stray waif whose parentage was doubtful.

Out of school, George improved the time by studying at night, so that when he returned to school he continued with his classes. His mother spent some of his earnings in candles, by the light of which he studied. She wanted him to be a scholar like her young massa, who went North to college and became convinced of the sin of slavery, though he never told any save herself of the fact. Ever after, he was her ideal, and the best the house afforded was brought out when he came home in vacation. She kept his secret deep down in her own heart. He was now a respected minister, and she loved and revered him. If her son was only like him, noble, manly and true, she would be thankful. In all her toil and trials she held up her young massa as one whose example could be safely followed.

As the freedmen advanced in means and intelligence they gave attention to their dress and homes. The rough shanties were cleaned up, and in many there was an air of neatness hitherto unknown. Through George's skillful hands a chimney was built in the end of their cabin, instead of having the fire in the center of the earth floor. The pine box, on which they ate their meals, had given way to a neat table. A set of knives and forks, a few dishes, with bits of carpet here and there over the rough floor, gave their room a comfortable, home-like appearance. Their limited room and few conveniences made it difficult for George to carry out his ideas of order. "A place for everything, and everything in its place," was his motto. So great was his desire for knowledge, that he saved every bit of newspaper and folded it away to read at his leisure.

This desire for knowledge seemed to be contagious. Other homes and neighborhoods were waking up to the importance of having schools. Application was made at the mission for a teacher for a school sixteen miles from the city. The wages offered were not much inducement, but George was selected for the place. Though young, he was manly and dignified in manner. His father, who was just out of prison, thought ten dollars a month small pay for a teacher. The mother, taking a more practical view of the subject, said:

"Half a loaf is better'n no bread. Look at me toilin' an' toilin' at de wash-tub an' iron-board from mornin' to night, an' cookin' fur de family. It would be a long time befo' I could make dat much."

"Yer better paid accordin' ter yer time," said her husband, who did not appreciate woman's work.

"I dunno; my work is nebbah done, an' I gits berry little fur it."

George heard this conversation. His mother's hard lot made him decide to go and teach. Mentally he was a rich man. Never before had he a prospect of so much money. He turned over in his mind how many nice things it would buy his mother. Among them he did not forget a large Bible. He had taught her to read, and she wanted one with large print, like ole massa's. "Then I must have a 'carpet bag' to hold my clothes, a hat and a pair of shirts." His mother drew a long breath when he told all his wants. She visited the mission store and procured the articles. There were hats of all kinds and styles, including Derbys and high silk hats. She turned them over and over again, and finally selected a high silk hat but little worn, promising to pay for it in "washin'."

George laughed as he held it up and asked what she got that for.

"Yer gwine ter be a teacher, an' mus' be 'spectable lookin'."

"It must be the cast-off hat of some big preacher. It will not add much to my looks, mother. See, it comes down over my eyes and ears. It has been some powerful man's hat."

"Reckon it was a preacha's."

George turned it and read a name on the inside lining.

"What's dat yo' readin' 'bout my young massa, George?"

"Why, yes, mother; his name is on the inside," said he, reading the name aloud."

"I declah I likes dat hat, cos it looks jes like him when he used ter cum home 'cation times."

The hat reminded her of her massa, whom she loved, and she bought and brought it home. It was a pardonable ambition in her to look and be like the good.

"Where did you get such a big hat?"

said his teacher, when George called to
get directions to his school.

"Mother took a fancy to it and
bought it. I wore it to please her."

His teacher examined and found one
corresponding with his clothes, and
which George accepted in place of the
other.

After bidding his teacher farewell, he
picked up his carpet bag and started on
foot to his school.

CHAPTER IV.

It was a calm, clear morning in April. A rain storm had passed over the day before, making the air stiff and breezy. The sun shone brightly on the glistening grass at the roadside; fleecy clouds flitted across the clear, blue sky, and the little birds warbled their sweetest notes. All nature was springing into life under the genial atmosphere of this delightful spring morning. George was buoyant with hope on the morning he left his humble home to go and try to teach school. A feeling of self-importance came over him, and he wondered if he could see his cabin in the north of town. Reaching the highest point on

5

the road he laid down his carpet bag,
and looking back over the city the first
building he saw was the handsome marble State House. It never looked so large
as it did this morning, as he stood
gazing at it in admiration. The re-
flected light of the sun on the stained
glass windows suggested what he read
of speeches by Andrew Johnson and
others inside those walls when slavery
was the exciting theme. What a
change, thought he; that subject no
longer troubles the statesmen. He
looked in every direction, and there
were places yet visible telling sad stories
of war and decay. Over to the right
he could see the breastworks thrown up
by General Thomas before his battle
with Hood. For the first time he had
a realizing sense of the horrors of war.

Was all that blood shed for poor, black boys like me?   How many noble young men gave their lives that I and others might be free!   Raising his eyes toward heaven he promised, God helping, to live and labor for the good of his race. Happy in his new resolution he gathered up his carpet bag and proceeded on his journey.

A few miles from the city he came to a charming country seat, "with closed doors, from which life and thought have gone away," once the home of a rich slaveholder, who spared no pains or slave labor in improving the grounds. Since the war the house had fallen into decay. Pieces of fine statuary, evidences of former wealth and glory, were still standing here and there like sentinels over the grounds. He had

heard his father tell of grand old country seats, where people lived in splendid
ease, but he did not expect to find one
so near home.   This wealthy planter,
like others, went abroad and copied
after the English.   A rustic seat near
by afforded a resting place, and sitting
down he looked long at that once magnificent but now deserted home.

Evidences of war and devastation
were everywhere before him.   At last
saddened by the view and growing
weary, he started up again and went
on until he came to a little stream
gushing out of the splendid limestone
rock, and coursing its way down the
side of the hill and spreading out over
the banks.   Here seating himself beside
this beautiful stream he ate the lunch
his mother had so kindly provided.

As he opened the gay bandana he thought of her kindness and love; how all her life she cared for his comfort. Now that she was making great sacrifices for his education, would he ever be able to repay her?

The sun was sinking behind the western hills, as he came near the place where he was to open his first school. He inquired at a house about the way. A half dozen curly heads rushed to the door, all so eager to tell him, that he was compelled to ask them to stop; and when they were quiet, he asked the largest boy to direct him.

"Go ober dar, by Jack's shop, an' when yer cum ter Mass Fry's, den go down ter a creek, en go ober it, en yo's dar, sah."

This was about as indefinite as anything George had ever heard about roads; but it was not likely he could find anyone more capable of directing him, so he followed it as well as he could. Coming to the creek he asked a colored man for Cross Creek school house.

"Ober dar," pointing to a low cabin. "Is yer de teachah?"

When told that he was, the man invited him into his home, and he was cordially welcomed by the hostess, a large, fat woman, who soon had a good supper on the table, and the stranger was invited to "set up."

George felt safe when he lay down that night, for he was with people who feared "de Lawd." He would have but little opportunity for study, as he was expected to board among the scholars.

Early Monday morning he was at the school house, a cabin seated with rough benches and stools. The children commenced coming, and continued to come all day. Punctuality was a thing they never had been taught. It was necessary at the beginning to enforce some very strict rules. Parents as well as children needed training in habits of punctuality. The discipline of the school in Nashville was laid down and most vigorously enforced. Though young, he had good command over the scholars. He wanted it to be a model school. It would be hard to describe the motley throng which crowded into that room, all anxious to see "de young teachah." It was wonderful to see a colored man acting like white folks. Some walked five miles, and

crossed marshy ground, bare-footed and
bare-headed, and with but little clothing on their bodies.

There were coarse, bad boys, who
bragged that they drank whiskey, and
were guilty of unmentionable sins.
There was some low grumbling among
them, when the teacher told them that
the first boy who should spit on the
floor should take a mop and wipe it up,
and that for the second offense, he
would be kept after school.

Order and neatness were taught, and
above all truthfulness and honesty,
essential traits in building up character.
For lack of these there were many de-
formed characters among them. To
impress these immortal souls with the
exceeding sinfulness of sin, and that
for every transgression they would be

punished, was a difficult task. He loved his Bible; it was his guide. He tried to comprehend its meaning, as he studied it from day to day and read from its pages. No book interested the children so much as the Bible. They never tired reading or hearing it read. A solemn awe came over them when he commenced reading from its pages. The histories of Joseph, David and Esther were specially attractive to them. When held up as models the scholars would say:

"No use: dey is white folks; we can't be like 'em."

When told that God had made of one blood all nations and was no respecter of persons, they looked in blank astonishment.

Thus by his reading and study of the

Bible he was being prepared for the
great work before him.   His experience
as a teacher gave him an insight into
the sad effects of slave life.   To his
eye the scars of slavery were ever
visible.   The ignorance of parents
could be seen in the dwarfed intellects
of their children.   Now and then one
gave evidence of unusual aptness in
acquiring knowledge, but the average
intelligence of his scholars was below
what he expected.   His keen sense of
right, and his religious education were
developing much that was good and
useful in him, and made him willing
and anxious to impart it to others.
Few could read or write; their ignorance was indeed deplorable.   Their
preachers, in whose judgment they
placed implicit confidence as leaders,

were unfit for their positions as teachers
and leaders.

At the close of his term George, full
of hope, prepared to return to his home.
The clouds which darkened his path-
way were being dispelled, and he was
not aware of the cheering news that
awaited him. A kind gentleman from
the North had been to see his parents,
and had arranged to send him to a
northern college, and pay for his education. This was a pleasant surprise, for
his ambition was to find something to
do by which he could get an education.
Providence now opened the way and
furnished the means, so he could go
through his course without delay. He
now prepared for college.

We will not ask the reader to follow
him over all those years which were

spent most industriously in the prose-
cution of his studies.   Suffice it to say,
at their close his perseverance was rewarded by the faculty conferring upon
him the first honors of his class.   As a
scholar and gentleman he had no peer
in the college, and he was withal a
devoted Christian.

He was now prepared for his life
work; but before settling down to this
he would visit his brethren in Washington City.

CHAPTER V.

GEORGE VISITS WASHINGTON

" The greatest men of the world are those who have
been able to sway by moral and spiritual forces stars in the
firmament, and beacon lights on shore."

George had long cherished a plan for
visiting the Capital City, and seeing
where grand statesmen distinguished
themselves speaking in behalf of freedom. He also wanted to see what
progress his people had made since
their freedom. In these days of speedy
travel, he was not long accomplishing
the journey. While enjoying the
changing scenery, he was studying the
faces of his fellow-passengers. Some
of them made him feel uncomfortable
on account of his color. This was no-

ticeable in trains, and hotels, and wherever brought in contact with white people. His first-class ticket was no protection from the insults of those who gathered up their skirts in horror, because compelled to ride in the same coach, and sit in the same seat, with a negro. He was very sensitive to such treatment, and could not see why an intelligent colored man should not receive as polite treatment as a rude beer-guzzler at his side, whose breath and clothing were fairly saturated with liquor and tobacco.

An agreeable incident showed that he was not without friends, even among the most refined ladies. He had gone out at a station for lunch, leaving his satchel on the floor instead of the seat. When he returned he found in his seat

a big aristocratic man with a red face,
that grew redder as George proceeded
to take his seat beside him. The man
scolded at the insolence of "niggers"
expecting to ride with white people, but
George said nothing in reply. The
passengers heard all and were annoyed. A lady sitting near offered him
a seat at her side. He thanked her
with all the politeness of a well-bred
gentleman, and took the seat so kindly
offered. This raised a titter among the
passengers, whose sympathies were
with the would-be aristocrat in his ideas
of negro equality. The good lady at
once entered into conversation with
him. She was a judge of character and
could not be mistaken in regard to his
respectability.

With wise tact she let him know that

6

she was interested in his race, and labored and spent means for their elevation, both North and South. Her's
was one of the oldest and most respectable Quaker families in Philadelphia, and she spent her time in philan-
thropic work. She was much interested as George unfolded his history
and plan of visiting Washington and
looking into the moral, social and physi-
cal condition of his people.

"You will find a sad state of things
among some of your people," she said.
"Intemperance, impurity and every
evil example are leading many of them
to destruction. Designing men are
taking advantage of their weakness and
many of them are being hopelessly
ruined. It is done so quietly that only

those laboring in reform fully under-
stand and realize it."

She had scarcely finished her remarks when the train stopped at her
station. George assisted her with her
baggage, while she put a bill in his
hand, he all the time wondering at his
singular good fortune.

He had prayed for something to do
to help him along, and it came in this
way. He was being prepared for trials
awaiting him.

It was on a warm, sultry morning
that he first set foot in the capital. He
had often heard of this beautiful city of
"magnificent distances," now he realized the truth as he stood at the head
of Pennsylvania avenue looking down
as far as the eye could reach. On in-
quiring for a hotel kept by people of

his color, he was directed to one on
Fourteenth street, but on going there
he found, to his great disappointment,
it was no place for him. The proprie-
tor kindly informed him that his house
was kept for white folks, members of
Congress and other regular boarders,
who were decidedly opposed to asso-
ciating with colored people.

His cheeks burned with shame when
he heard this. Was he not an educated man, sober and well behaved?
Why such distinction at the seat of a
republican government? Was it consistent for a colored man to encourage
caste? This caste problem was harder
than any he had found at college.
Who would, could or should solve it?
After walking miles in search of a resting place, and growing tired and hun-

gry, he entered Temple Cafe, on Ninth street, but the elegance of the place made him afraid to ask for something to eat. It was kept by a white lady, who received him kindly and gave him a table all to himself, and colored servants served him a good breakfast. This cafe was kept on temperance principles, and the boarders were among the most respectable women and men in office, and others visiting the city temporarily and otherwise. This Christian lady presided over the cuisine, trained her servants to be useful citizens, and labored for the promotion of temperance among the colored people of the District, and was beloved for her interest in them. All in her employ were taught that truthfulness and honesty were essential to good character.

After breakfast George started out to
view the city. Dog days are not the
most favorable for making good impres-
sions on those visiting the capital for
the first time. The sun's rays pouring
down on marble and granite and re-
flected from asphalt streets added to
the discomfort of sight-seeing.

With it all a somber cloud hung over
the capital at this time. President Jas.
A. Garfield, whose voice had often
been heard in defense of justice, had
been smitten by cruel hands, and lay
in the White House, just before being
taken to Elberon. His life fast ebbing
away, he was carefully watched, and
each change in his condition heralded
to every part of this and other lands.
Men, women and children walked and
talked softly during those sorrowful

days. People met in churches and prayed : " God spare our President." Then came days alternating between hope and despair. Only a few months ago President Garfield had been sworn into office in the presence of thousands. Now he lay dying. In his delirium he talked of the sea ; if he were only beside it, health would come again. They carried him there ; recovery was not so decreed. One evening, while the people all over the land were praying that he might be spared, the noble life went out. It was a beautiful evening in September, 1881. George was returning from church where prayers were offered for the dying President. He had hardly reached his lodging place when the tolling bells took up the sad refrain— the martyr President is no more.

Then came trying days, waiting for the body to be brought back from El-beron. At last the funeral train arrived with the remains. These lay for three days in state in the rotunda of the Capitol. Men, women and children from far and near came, some to look for the first, all for the last time on the murdered President. The middle aged and young, and those who were bowed with the infirmities of age, whites and blacks, came. None were more interested spectators than the colored people, many of whom on the funeral day walked ten and fifteen miles, and stood in the hot sun all day in the procession which reached many squares. Poor old men and women hobbled along, and as they passed the coffin dropped silent tears. One old woman, bent with age,

stooping down as she passed to better
see the face, said audibly: " Poah fellow, how he mus' hev suffe'd," so ema-
ciated was his face.

> " The old, the young, the grave, the gay,
>   Were bowed alike in grief."

Only fifteen hundred persons were
admitted to the rotunda to attend the
funeral obsequies.   These, the highest
officials, and foreign ministers, and am-
bitious politicians recently at swords'
points, that day forgot the past, and,
arm in arm, walked together and min-
gled their tears over the untimely death
of their President.   But no colored man
was there.   Guitteau, the miserable as-
sassin, was trembling in his prison cell
for a crime committed on an unoffend-
ing brother, for which he should sooner

have been brought to account. Not
until he expiated his crime on the gal-
lows was the law vindicated. Then the
nation breathed freely again.

The funeral over, amid strains of delightful music by the Marine Band, they
bore him who was honored in life, and
still more in death, to the train which
carried him to his last resting place in
Cleveland, Ohio.

Men were detailed as guards to protect the body that no harm overtake it
by the way. Sad that with that train
liquor in large quantity was sent for
those who wished to use it, but no one
was detailed to look after it, or its con-
sequences. Afterward bills were presented to Congress, and voted to be
paid, of eight thousand dollars, ex-
penses for liquors used at the funeral

and the Yorktown centennial. George
was in the gallery and heard the bill
discussed. He thought what a fine opportunity this to display a little tact
and courage. Would no one oppose
this unjust bill? Where were the
heroic men who pleaded so fearlessly
for freedom? Are they not needed to
plead for those bound down by the
cruel drink habit?

As he listened to the discussion of
this unjust bill he thought if that was
what statesmen called political economy he wanted to hear no more of it.
He congratulated himself that no colored man had anything to do in this dis-
graceful affair, except, perhaps, to
serve the liquors on the train.

Like most of his race, George was
naturally religious. He was a close ob-

server of all that was going on around
him. He read of balls and dances
soon after the funeral. He thought
how wicked and irreverent. One day a
nation in tears, the next reveling and
dancing. Even long-established custom
could not make it right in his eyes.
Just before Lent twenty-four consecu-
tive balls were announced to take place
in Masonic Hall the next twenty-four
week nights. The usual accompani-
ments of the ball room were there.
He rejoiced that his people would not
be permitted to attend, even if they desired to ; but it was possible that some
of them would serve "refreshments."
It was so; the rattle of glasses and bottles falling below, told the story.
Colored men were actually serving the
dancers with liquors, and throwing the

empty glasses and bottles in an alley below.

The habits of some of those waiters could be traced to the example of officials. Was it surprising they wanted to be there? There was money to be made, and they could hear enchanting music. The Cabinet officer, with his eight thousand dollar salary, was there; and the Government clerk, whose salary was hardly sufficient to pay his board. The gambler and libertine were there, and men and women who loved pleasure and extravagant display. The example there was far-reaching in its influence. Colored, as well as whites, were being lured to ruin by this example. What would become of his people, sixty-five thousand of whom lived at the capital? They were poor, and

by many despised. They were sur-
rounded by every temptation and diffi-
culty. A few men had become wealthy.
Hon. Fred. Douglass and Mr. Wormly
had acquired wealth amounting to hun-
dreds of thousands of dollars. Their
advantages for education were good.
They had their schools and private
seminaries, and some, like their aristocratic white neighbors, sent their sons
and daughters abroad to be educated.
Already signs of caste were visible, the
better educated and wealthy being un-
willing to associate with the poor and
ignorant. Many were indolent and
shiftless, living from hand to mouth in a
sort of dreamy way, believing, hoping
" Suthin would turn up by 'm by."

It troubled George to see so many
bright men in positions in hotels and

saloons, where their morals were in danger. Intelligent Africans in Washington, as elsewhere, accepted white apron and tea towel positions, when, by a little perseverance and energy, they could have fitted themselves for something better and more ennobling. Their white neighbors decided their fitness to serve. It did not require much education, and they accepted their positions in all humility. Few had the energy and ambition of John M. Langston, Mr. Bruce and Fred. Douglass, who fought their way up to fame and fortune by hard study. George wished that more of his race had a desire for knowledge. He saw too many idle, vicious-looking men out of employment begging on the streets, stopping pedestrians to tell of want and suffering.

7

Like hungry office seekers, they came
to the capital when Congress met to
"gather crumbs from Uncle Sam's
table." They were not hard to satisfy,
for a few pennies generally sufficed to
bring a hearty "thankee," and they
passed on to repeat the same story to
the next whom they met. This habit
of begging they learned from the Sisters of Charity, who gathered money
by the thousands every year in ten cent
bits from clerks in office, ostensibly to
build asylums for children.

George found the black man not behind the white one about using tobacco.
Men were inveterate smokers and chew-
ers. Outside the market house women
could be seen crouching down beside
little fires smoking their cob pipes, and
selling tobacco "twist."

"Have some 'backer'?" was asked of all who passed their way. When spoken to about it they said : "White folks smoke. I'm gwine to be like 'em. We is mighty imitative creeters."

Passing along Massachusetts avenue one day, he heard slow but plaintive music. As he came near he decided they were playing a funeral march. It was a procession of colored men in the grotesque dress of some order, marching to the grave of one of their comrades. Their training in wearing white aprons made them specially graceful in that role ; but their dilapidated hats and bedraggled white plumes suggested cast-off finery, and he queried, "When will my people quit aping the whites in their small clothes ?"

CHAPTER VI.

MRS. HAYES' EXAMPLE.

" Who is the moral hero ? It is the woman who is willing to encounter odium and scorn, obloquy and contempt in doing what is right.''

Wherever George went he was treated as an inferior. In the street cars, at the Capitol, or in crowds, the same " stand aside, I am better than thou " policy prevailed. He resolved to test the matter fully before leaving the city by attending the President's reception. Word was out as to its cosmopolitan character, all nationalities and classes in society being invited. On the evening of this reception for the people, en masse, our hero joined the great throng which slowly wended its way up in front of the White House. He was alone on his tour of observation, and, coming near, his heart beat quickly, for he would soon know whether he would be permitted to mingle socially with whites at the reception. He had not proceeded far after entering, when a policeman touched him on the shoulder and informed him that he could not be admitted.

"On what grounds, sir?" asked George, somewhat excitedly.

"Color," said the policeman.

George was a noble-looking man, and straightening up to his full stature, and speaking volumes out of his keen black eyes, he proceeded to lay down the new code of etiquette for receptions.

"You have admitted Foreign Ministers, sir?" said he with an enquiring look.

"Yes," said the man in the blue coat.

"Are not Chinese colored?"

The policeman was obliged to confess.

"Where is the consistency? I am an American citizen and voter, sir, born and educated that all men are equal. You exclude me because I belong to a poor, oppressed people, long trodden down. My education makes me aspire to something noble. I have a higher destiny. I want to be a man, a part of this great company, who delight in honoring the President, who has honored my people. I want equality. In law it is just and right."

"What do you mean?" asked the officer in an imperious manner.

"Mr. Arthur, sir, defended a colored woman who was ejected from the street cars in New York, and gained the suit, sir. Ever since colored people ride in the cars with white folks. He did it when it was very unpopular. I want to see and pay my respects to a man of such principles."

"Go in," said the officer; "but you will run the risk of being snubbed."

"I shall run the risk, sir," said George with a triumphant air.

The next encounter was with the officer who stood by, and introduced the President as the people passed. The first question asked, was:

"Are you a foreigner?"

"No, sir, American."

"How came you here?"

"I am a voter, a citizen of this free country, sir."

"We don't recognize the equality of
negroes here.   You are excused."

The President seeing George's em-
barassment, reached out his hand and
giving it a cordial grasp, beckoned him
on into the parlor.

The first thing that attracted his attention in this room was Mrs. Hayes'
portrait, standing on the floor, leaning
against the wall.   It was set in a massive
wood frame, handsomely carved by
ladies in Cincinnati.   The portraits of
George and Martha Washington were in
full view as he entered the blue parlor.
He remembered hearing that Mrs.
Hayes' portrait was not permitted to be
hung permanently beside theirs ; and he
wondered why they objected ! Was she
not as deserving of honor as Martha
Washington ? Was not her example

more worthy of imitation? She had the moral courage to banish liquors from the White House during the four years she was mistress of it. She set an example before her children and the youth of this century, which the colored people could safely follow. She deserved to have her name engraved in letters of gold in the State dining room, as a memorial of her, for banishing a useless and dangerous custom from the White House.

George woke from his reverie in time to see one whom the nation delighted to honor, make his appearance. Wherever he went, all eyes followed, intent on seeing, while many waited to take the hand of General Grant, who led our armies, and brought freedom to the enslaved. Women as well as men were ready to do him homage. George thought they forgot that the God of battles, whose ear heard the cry of the down-trodden and oppressed, was their deliverer, and had answered their prayers. A feeling of gratitude filled his heart, as he recalled all that had been done in gaining freedom to his race. He was thankful for the silent influence of her whose portrait stood on the floor, in the Green Room. Was she not *really* the first lady of the land? Her example should make her as dear to the colored people as freedom itself. If followed by them, there would be no drunkenness among them. When they visit the White House, how pleasant it will be to tell the beautiful story to their children of Mrs. Hayes' refusing to set liquors before her guests.

The next place he visited was the Capitol and the restaurant in the basement. He was not favorably impressed with the *example* of many who frequented those places. Waiters told him half confidentially that large quantities of liquors were used by Congressmen in those restaurants. A smart mulatto, in the Senate restaurant, gave a significant smile when asked,

"If liquors were much used."

"Oh, yes, when they are sick."

Judging from what he saw and heard, some of them were often very sick.

The next place we find George seated in the gallery assigned to colored men, listening to the speeches on the tariff. Soon the tobacco smoke came rolling up from the House of Representatives so strong that he was compelled to leave

and go down to the reception room ; but
this was so elegant with its marble floor
that he was afraid to stop there. A
gentleman came into the room who forgot
to remove his hat. An officer ordered
him to take it off. The code of etiquette
at the Capitol did not embrace enough.
There were ladies present whose nerves
were much more shocked with the
smoking than with the hat that man
forgot to remove.

Sick and disgusted, George went
down stairs, pondering as he went, as to
how far his people were guilty in culti-
vating the tobacco habit. The handsome
marble floor and stairs were so stained
with tobacco that he concluded Congress
could not do a better thing than to ap-
propriate money for an annex for a
smoking room eight stories up, so that

visitors and others who do not smoke, would not be annoyed with it. It was with some relief that he reached the door and breathed the pure air of heaven again.

A few rods from the Capitol, drinking places and houses of infamy were carrying on their wicked business. Was it surprising that women all over the land went out in a crusade against these evils when the brightest statesmen and wisest men were being lured to ruin ?

George was a conscientious man, he feared God and kept his commandments. It hurt him to see and know that men would disgrace their constituency and those who gave them positions by frequenting such places. He went to his lodging with a heavy heart. His insight into the sins and temptations of

8

political life made him fearful for the
future of his race. Could they take
part in politics and not be corrupted?
What incentive had they to be statesmen, when so many of those of whom
one would expect better things, go
astray?

CHAPTER VII.

CABINET DINNER.

" God give us men !   A time like this demands
  Great hearts, strong minds, true faith and willing hands;
  Men whom the lust of office does not kill;
  Men whom the spoils of office cannot buy,
  Men who possess opinions and a will;
  Men who have honor, men who cannot lie;
  For while the rabble with their thumbscrew creeds,
  Their large professions and their little deeds,
  Wrangle in selfish strife—lo ! Freedom weeps,
  Wrong rules the land, and waiting Justice weeps."
                                    —O. W. Holmes.

The next morning after George's visit to the Capitol, he was out bright and early, having promised to assist a waiter at a cabinet dinner, to be given that evening by a member of the cabinet to members of the cabinet and their families.   All were anxious that this reception should excel the previous one.

None entered into the spirit of the occasion with a heartier zest than the waiters. There was always a charm about everything done and said among society people during Congress that pleased the waiters. The last dinner was such a charming affair ! Could it ever be excelled ? Efficient servants had much to do in making receptions pleasant; many of them being fine caterers, and skillful in giving the finishing touches to the tables, arranging plants, flowers, etc.

George was a genius, helpful as a waiter, equally at home demonstrating a problem in mathematics or conjugating a Latin verb. A house of so much beauty and grandeur as this was in strange contrast with most homes he had ever seen, North and South. Soon

guests in glittering equipages arrived
with gay and happy people, who were
welcomed by the host and hostess in
the spacious parlors. The usual com-
pliments of the season and social conversation occupied the time until dinner
was served at nine o'clock, the hour
long looked for by the anxious servants.
As the guests entered the dining room
the band struck up a beautiful march.
The room was brilliant with flowers
whose fragrance filled the air. It was
like a scene in a fairy tale.

The table was spread for forty, and
at each plate were six glasses, turned
down. This did not escape George's
notice; but he was so bewildered
with the pomp and grandeur of the
affair that he almost forgot where he
was. The company took their seats,

but no thanks were offered the Giver of
all good for blessings bestowed. Twelve
courses were served in the most approved style, and after two hours and a
half's surfeit of good things, their glasses
were turned up and six kinds of wine
passed around.   Host and hostess,
gentlemen and ladies, matrons and
maidens partook, but few refused the
sparkling cup.   They became merry
and merrier, their eyes grew brighter,
their laughter louder, and amid the
clinking of glasses and music, all left
the table.

The rest of the evening was spent by
the ladies in examining the charming
trosseau of the lovely Mrs. Blank,
whose beautiful daughter quite carried
off the palm at the piano, while the
gentlemen discussed the next election

and the bill for the improvement of the Potomac Flats. At 1 A. M. the company retired, as they came, except they now made more noise.

The waiters were silent observers of all that was done and said during the time of serving, but after all was over they had their remarks and criticisms.

George improved the occasion by giving them a lecture on the dangers of handling and using liquors. He had not violated his principles by serving them, and could with greater propriety pronounce a woe on those who "put the bottle to their neighbors' mouth."

"I am not surprised that so many fall before temptation, when they are forced to smell and serve liquors to the whites," said he afterwards.

All the reply he could get was:

"Dar's no use'n trublin' yo' self, dey's boun' ter hev it ebbery time, sah."

Such poor fellows would follow the example of those who put on style, no matter if it ruined them.

The grey of morning had made its appearance before he retired from the festive scene. Hurrying along the street to his lodging, he was suddenly overtaken by an officer who asked him to go with him into a low tumble-down tenant house. Seeing light, and hearing a noise inside, he entered. The officer led him along a narrow passage and up a rickety stairway, and brought him face to face with a scene of a different character from the one he had just witnessed.

The room was small, bare of furniture, only a broken chair or two, and a bed on which lay a colored woman in the last stages of consumption. On the floor, beside her, lay her only son, in a drunken stupor, with a half empty whiskey bottle at his side. He came home crazed with drink, and struck his dying mother because she would not rise and get him something to eat. A kind neighbor, hearing her groans, came in, in time to save her life. After providing for the poor woman, and assisting the officer in getting the intoxicated man out of the house, George proceeded on his way. He was turning over in his mind all the different scenes of the night, when all at once he saw a man, with arm stretched out, over a colored man who was kneeling at his feet. For a moment he forgot where he was. It was the Lincoln monument. The figure with outstretched arm was the noble man who proclaimed freedom to the slave. George's first impulse was to bow before him, as the marble slave, but there came welling up into his heart strange, unwelcome thoughts. Was freedom a myth? Were colored people really free? Were they not bound down by a more cruel bondage, learned from white folks' customs and habits? Could they ever free themselves from these?

Why should a colored man bow down before a white man for doing his duty? Was it not a fearful legacy that the white man was leaving them? Freedom to do as they please—drink, murder, steal and be imprisoned—freedom to degrade their wives and little children; freedom to drink with statesmen and men in high places, robbing them of their God-given Sabbaths, by turning

EMANCIPATION

A RACE SET FREE
AND THE COUNTRY AT PEACE
LINCOLN
RESTS FROM HIS LABORS

BRAGDON PITTS. PA.

this holy day into one of business and pleasure, thus compelling his people to break it. Would they ever do right with such example before them?

Though the outlook at Washington was not as bright as he could have wished, still he was satisfied that progress had been made in educational matters. Their educated ministers were doing a good work in leading to purer thoughts, and encouraging a desire for greater knowledge. Too little was being done, however, to educate the masses on the subject of temperance, gambling, etc. As a result, there was suffering and poverty among them. When Congress was in session, many colored people could be seen in the gallery, listening attentively, catching up everything said. They were as good

listeners as many whites who frequented
the galleries.

George rather enjoyed watching and
studying the cranky-looking men and
women going in and out of the galleries.
Women and men with long hair and
short, came rushing in to get seats.
Among them was one who made yearly
pilgrimages to the Capitol whose face
had grown so familiar that the colored
people watched him with suspicion, because he dressed well, but had no visible
means of support. In his own estimation,
Congress could not get on without his
presence.

The reporters came with self-important
air and took the seats allotted them. It
was worth a journey there, to see those
hailing from "the Hub." The airs they
put on! A lady with pad and pencil in

hand, took her seat in the reserved gallery. From the decided look on her face she must be entrusted with an important work and will not be frustrated in it.

The session was half gone before members were ready for business, and even then, many were absent. Senators were about to discuss a Memorial bill for a Commission of inquiry into the nature and effeɑs of the alcoholic liquor traffic.

Bill 900 on the calendar, was called for and discussed pro and con, quite satisfactory it seemed to the speakers. The friends of the bill were nearly all Northern men, and when the vote was taken, twenty-six Republicans, six Democrats and two Independents voted for the Commission. A member of the House, who was in the Senate, said to

9

a Senator: " You can afford to vote for that bill, it will be killed in the House." And so it was.

Before leaving Washington, George accepted an invitation to a party given by a colored club of young men, to which young women were also invited. The company was very select, only a limited number being invited. The men were in full dress, and the women wore low-necked dresses and short sleeves. The code of their aristocratic white neighbors was followed to the letter, two hours and a half being spent at the table.   George was not surprised at seeing five glasses at each plate, and five kinds of liquor on the sideboard, which were served to all present except George and a young lady, who had too much principle to break their pledge.

All the rest drank once and again until they were more or less intoxicated, one woman having to remain over night to sleep off her drunken stupor. George left disgusted at what he had seen and heard, and as his thoughts turned toward his Southern home, he wondered if his people there were being lured to ruin as were these in the North.

CHAPTER VIII.

HOMEWARD BOUND.

" Go to thy mother's side,
    And her crushed spirit cheer;
Thine own deep anguish hide,
    Wipe from her cheek the tear."

George left Washington for the South
land with a less hopeful feeling than
when he arrived there. He knew more
of public life, and the true inwardness
of men, especially politicians, and had
less respect for statesmen generally.
While the train bore him rapidly toward
his Southern home, he was deeply impressed with the visible fact that the
South was far behind the North in im-
provements which he very justly traced
to the blighting effects of slavery. What

incentive had slaves to build up a country
when they were bowed down, wronged
and poorly fed? The South, with all its
inexhaustible natural resources, is but
poorly developed; but now, with remun-
erated labor, the freed men should raise
twice as much grain and cotton as they
did in slavery, and do their work better.
What is needed is willing hearts and
hands to make the South land an Eden
of beauty. Their work will always be
needed to dig coal and raise corn and
cotton, and if all able to work have fair
wages promptly paid, they will acquire
homes and be happy.

He was so absorbed with his thoughts
that he did not notice that he was near-
ing his old home. Soon he would see
his kind mother, from whom he had
been long separated. All the colored

people of the neighborhood knew of the arrival of the distinguished guest. No sooner had he stepped from the platform than he was greeted in the old time, cordial manner, by hosts of friends. There were some exceptions. Idle, envious ones who never had energy enough to do or be anything useful, stood back, watching everything he did. His brother met him and hurried him home to meet the faithful mother who was waiting to welcome her long absent son. George noticed with pride the comfort and neatness of everything around the humble home. On the right of the walk leading to the door, were many pretty flowers, while on the left was a little garden of vegetables of the season. The white spread on the bed in the sitting room was rivalled only by the snowy white pillows and clean cloth on the table on which was spread a nice, warm breakfast ready to be served.

It was a plain meal compared with many he had enjoyed since leaving home, but there were precious memories here which no other place could have for him. Here was the devoted mother who met him with open arms, saying, "De Lawd is kind an' good ter me, yer home agin. Sit down dar, honey, an' make yo'self at home. Ise so glad to see yer. Is yer well? How well yer look." She was proud of him. She had prayed that he would grow up a useful man like his namesake, and she now believed her prayer was answered. She loved to see all her children doing well, and now that he whom she had dedicated to special work, was home again, she was supremely happy.

Hard work providing for her family, had made her old and stiff, but she had a cheerful heart and was contented with her lot. She wept as she offered George the vacant seat by her side at the table. All the legacy her husband left was a drunkard's wife. A shade of sadness came over George's face, for since he left home his father had died a drunkard, and left him the legacy of shame. The habit of taking his bitters was learned from his old master and physician, and no influence could change him. To the last he quoted their example and Paul's injunction to Timothy, "Take a little wine for the stomach's sake and thine often infirmities."

The mother was strictly temperate and had impressed her character on her children, who were sober and upright men, respected for their honesty and industry. George learned for the first time to whom he was indebted for his scholarship and education. Her young but now old Massa George furnished the means to pay his board and tuition at college.

He and his mother often spoke of God's goodness in providing so bountifully for all their wants since their freedom.

After spending a few days very pleasantly with his mother, he proceeded to Georgia, where he expected for the present to make his home. Before reaching his destination he had heard of the exciting temperance campaign going on in that state. An "amendment" to the Constitution prohibiting the manufacture and sale of liquors, except for medicinal, mechanical and sacramental purposes, had been submitted by the legislature to the people, for approval or rejection.

CHAPTER IX.

With purpose strong and steady,
  In the great Jehovah's name,
We rise to save our kindred,
  From a life of woe and shame;
And the Jubilee of freedom
  To slaves of sin proclaim.
Our God is marching on.
                    —Dr. Hunter.

A MILLION AND A HALF OF VOTERS.

George came on the stage at the most interesting time. Friends urged him to enlist in the work and use the gifts with which his Maker had endowed him. Believing that it was a contest for that which involved much to his race, he gave himself unreservedly to the "Amendment" campaign. Many a contest he had with the foes of the Amendment. Some objected that this

was the white man's war; blacks had
nothing to do with it. Professed
Christians were responsible for their
being brought to this country; professed
Christians held and sold them as slaves.
True Christians would now have to free
them from the slavery to rum. George
was not long in telling them that all he
wanted was their help in freeing the
South and with it, themselves, from the
saloon. Then they would advance.

" What had we to do in introducing
drinking customs, anyway? " asked one
of the more intelligent ones. " We were
brought to this country to be slaves and
were kept in slavery two hundred years,
and then had to fight for our freedom;
now we must turn around and fight the
liquor business. Why we had to raise
grain, run distilleries and furnish liquors
for this and other lands."

How sad that while they were doing this, men were bartering their souls and bodies to their appetites for rum.

George impressed upon all that they were not responsible for the past, but now were their own masters and should share the responsibilities of the whites. It was their duty as good citizens to help free the state and nation from the curse, and with it their own people, who were victims, no matter if it did compel them to undo what they did in slavery. The cruelty and oppression of slavery did not convince all that it was wrong and should be abolished; neither does the sin and danger of the drink traffic convince all now that liquor should be abolished; but it is the duty of those who have convictions, to agitate, as was done in time of slavery. George was willing to begin work on Southern soil. The whites needed all the help they could get, in the present campaign. There was a good chance for his people to distinguish themselves in helping to solve the liquor problem. Allowance would have to be made for their training of two hundred years, following the customs of whites. It would require time to undo this, but it was a satisfaction that his people were not guilty of introducing the drink custom. Those who came to the New World to found a pure government brought their habits with them. Seventeen years after the Puritans set foot on American soil, the first brewery was built. Side by side slavery and intemperance grew, until the sentiment was made which abolished the one and put the other on trial. It has been before

Congress for years and will continue to be until its destruction. The little germ of slavery planted in Jamestown, Va., spread and became an element of power by which kings and queens were ruled. Statesmen bowed down to it. That first brewery was the beginning of a business that has increased with years, and to-day is a mighty monied power, largely controlling political parties. The best men and women opposed the slave trade; but they were in the minority, just as the temperance folks are now. Brave men like Wilberforce, Garrison and Phillips, whose ears were always open to the cries of the oppressed, made the sentiment that more than all others helped to free the slave. Noble men and women, North and South, are now laboring to suppress the traffic in liquors.

10

George rejoiced that he was of the happy number, but it was a grief to him that so few of his people were willing to labor against that which he believed was their greatest enemy. Every day he was impressed that he had a work to do among those who, since their freedom, were becoming more and more intemperate.

His heart was touched with the misery and poverty on account of this. When men were in liquor they were bloodthirsty and revengful, always getting into trouble. It was hard to get the masses interested in the work. A dog fight was far more important, in their estimation, than a temperance meeting.

Georgia was the first State South to prohibit the importation of slaves from Africa. James Oglethorpe, a temperance man, when settling the first Georgia colony, pledged himself and followers to set their slaves free; so it was hoped that it would be the first in the galaxy of Southern States to free itself from the rum slavery. For this George was anxious to labor. He found many among the freedmen who were opposed to having their liberty taken away. Deep down in his own heart was a desire that God would raise up some one among his people to be a leader in this reform. Nothing would please him better than to "come to the kingdom for such a time as this," but he would wait and see what Providence had in store for him.

"If yer keep on agitatin' der liquor question I reckon dey will be anothah wah, sah," said one of the cowardly ones.

"Don't speak of it," said George, with a troubled look. "If our race do their duty they can save the Nation from this sin. Do you know that we have a million and a half of voters now in the South? Our votes will give us influence, but we must be careful."

"What if yer don't git de chance to cast yer ballot?" asked Percy Jones, who stopped to listen to the conversation.

"We must see to that, when the time comes," said George, with a shrug of his shoulders.

"Ise allus sad ter think of poor John Brown's end, all fur our sakes," said Percy, wiping away a tear.

"It was very sad, Percy, but he made a mistake to try to get up an insurrection among the slaves and to capture Harper's Ferry. Poor man, he wanted to free us, and paid dearly for violating the law. Ten persons, including his two sons and himself, lost their lives by it. He was a martyr, and his reckless act was overruled for our good. Much as slaves wanted liberty few were ready to join in an insurrection of that kind. I am proud that our folks were law abiding and faithful to their masters' families when left in their charge. It was the highest compliment masters could pay their slaves, to leave all in their care when they went to fight the North. The slaves waited patiently, believing their God was marching on and that their redemption was near."

"If dat question could ha' bin settled widout the dreffel loss of life," said Percy with a sigh.

"You see that question had to be

settled by blood. During the war one of the poets wrote:

" Some things are worthless, others so good,
That nations who buy them, pay only in blood."

"An' a mighty sight of it was shed befo' de wah was oveh, sah."

"Yes, it was terrible; but in every period of the world's history differences have been settled by force of arms. Joshua and David led great armies. Victor Immanuel and Garibaldi, Washington and Grant. It is said that five billions of men have perished in war. One hundred and eighty-six thousand ex-slaves fought in the late civil war, and twenty thousand negroes in the Revolutionary war."

"Dey was fightin' foh de women and chillen."

"Negroes have fought in eighty battles in this country."

"Is dat so, Mars George? Yo' see white folks set us a mighty bad 'zample," saying this Percy gathered up his spade to go to work.

"Indeed they have," said George, "but we must help to bring about the good time predicted in the Bible when "Nations shall beat their swords into ploughshares and their spears into pruning-hooks, and men will learn war no more." Christ came to bring "peace on earth and good will to men." We are part of this Nation and should do something to shape its destiny. I long to see this beautiful South redeemed from the curse of liquor; to see manhood and womanhood restored to freedom from the love of drink. Then joy will come to all still suffering for our sakes. The bitter past will be forgotten in our effort to save one another. Then the cruel lynchings will cease from our land and all will live in peace."

George had scarcely ceased talking, when a man came in who told about a man who was torn from a jail in a public square of a Southern city and lynched in presence of applauding men, women and children. These repeated cases grieved George, who wanted protection to his people when they did right; but to take their lives without judge or jury was not fair. As citizens they had an inalienable right to be treated fairly. This would go far toward solving "the Negro problem." Some of the freedmen were easily influenced by designing politicians, and those who

could be flattered by promises were
always getting into trouble with political
demagogues. Every now and then sums
of money were being used in purchasing
their ballots. George tried to teach all
to imitate the good and avoid the evil,
and to be careful they do not become the
tools of bad men. He was too late.
Already wicked men were at work, and
it would be impossible to overthrow
their wicked plans. The lower class of
whites and blacks were enlisting on the
side of rum. Catholic priests were busy
dictating to the colored men how to vote.
These never cared for the colored
men until they had a vote. Jesuits ma-
nipulated the schools everywhere, pick-
ing out the most intelligent boys and
sending them to Rome to be educated,
then brought back as missionaries

to the freedmen. George thought it would be a good plan to send missionaries to his people and rescue them from the Catholic church, to which the majority of liquor sellers and drinkers belonged. To put their necks in the Roman yoke would be a backward step in their civilization, and the worst slavery the freedmen ever knew.

He was sorry for his brethren who had been lured into that church; he would go to them with the open Bible, the great charter of our liberty; and but for the priests it would be theirs also.

CHAPTER X.

AN EDUCATED MINISTRY NEEDED.

"What a divine work and mission—to protect the weak."

George wanted to visit a Mission School in Alabama. In order to do this and see the country, he went in a private conveyance. The land in places was swampy and broken; the trees were covered with a kind of Spanish moss which gave a wild, weird look to every thing along the way. He expected to see alligators lying around, and imagined he could see the fugitive slave, Henry Bibb, jumping from tree to tree, trying to escape the scent of bloodhounds. While he was wondering where

the people lived, the buggy stopped in
front of the Mission, called the "Prayer
House." Entering the cabin school, he
found a room full of women who had
met for prayer. They sang a plantation
song in a plaintive tone, then a woman
offered prayer, which was like the wail
of a heart bearing a great burden which
she was bringing to the Lord. As they
sang and prayed their bodies swayed
back and forth, as they made their un-
earthly sounds, groanings and gestures.

George talked to those mothers about
their duty to their children. They listened
with eyes and ears opened to all he had
to say to them. Their greatest need
was an educated ministry. The young
people in the mission schools refused
to hear ministers who would not inform
themselves in the gospel truths. It was

evident that if the colored people ever
became great leaders in that which
makes men and women noble and useful,
they should have some good example
before them. Their children in cities
needed the education to be had in the
public school the same as the children of
other nations. Contact with intelligent
white people would do them good. The
poor and rich of every white nation mingle
together in the public school, but the
poor despised Afro-American boy and
girl, no matter how gifted, are not
wanted. A moral and secular education
is needed by them and the poor whites,
whose ignorance can be traced to slavery.
The freedmen were thankful for the aid
government, churches and individuals
were giving to remove poverty and ignorance, but with it all there were bitter

complaints with their lot. Freedom was
sweet, but it had not improved their
circumstances as much as they expected.
The trials and crosses had not been
taken into the account, and many were
unhappy. George was humbled when
he remembered the privations many
suffered and still suffer, who gave dear
ones to free the land. Asylums and
homes for soldiers and orphans had
been liberally provided for those who
gave their services in the war. All he
asked was loyalty to the best government on earth, and that it would provide
as well for the orphans and widows
made by drink. He was thankful that
while government was maintaining its
honor, slavery went down, and he was
a free man.

CHAPTER XI.

PURITY IN HOME LIFE.

" Who can find a virtuous woman: for her price is far above rubies."—BIBLE.

There was a phase of social life among the freedmen which did not harmonize with George's ideas of propriety. So long taught to disregard the marriage relation, many now could see no harm in living in a sort of free-lover style, and there was no one to call them to account for it. At the close of the war there were sad revelations. Husbands and wives met, who had been separated years before and sold away so far that they married again and had families. Not only were they robbed of their earnings, but they were reduced to concubinage, and denied the civil rights of marriage. The nearest and dearest relationships were sundered, and prostitution encouraged. They were deprived of education, and especially of moral culture to teach them how to live. It was a penal offense to teach them to read. Parental authority was broken up by the domestic slave trade. Some slave owners never separated husbands and wives, or parents and children, but they were the exceptions. All had the legal right to do it. George taught all that the Bible condemned all separations except for one cause. It taught the sacredness of the relation which is for life. "What God hath joined together, let no man put asunder."

In going from place to place he found many men and women who needed to be lifted up out of the depths of vice and saved for lives of usefulness. There were poor intemperate women and men needing counsel and sympathy now as much as those did who were separated by cruel masters and the world is just as indifferent to their cries now as then. The voluntary but no less sinful slavery to appetite separates husbands and wives and children. It robs them of all earthly and heavenly hopes and fills the land with tramps.

George was becoming an enthusiastic reformer. While North, he made a special study of the temperance question. He delighted in tracing the analogy between this and slavery. He learned lessons in moral as well as political

11

economy. He thought that possibly
God had a purpose in freeing them at
the time. Was it that they might enlist
in the glorious warfare against the liquor traffic? He tried to keep in close
touch with the masses, if possible to win
them and aid in carrying the prohibitory
amendment. If it was lost and government would go on as in slavery
days, it might be left to the terrible al-
ternative of another war to suppress the
rum slavery. The thought of this made
George terribly in earnest, and all he
wanted was enough of men to carry the
amendment in Georgia.

As the time approached when it would
be decided, he was kept busy, having to
fill engagements to speak in many
towns and hamlets in the State. He was
developing the gift of oratory, and com-

manded the attention of some of the
cultured ones, who were forced to
accept his logic. When voting day arrived all interested were there to see
that justice was done and that colored
voters had a fair chance. Men worked
hard and cast ballots instead of bullets,
and gained the amendment.

There was great rejoicing that
Georgia was the first of the Southern
States to declare for prohibition. But
their joy was of short duration; owing
to some technicality, it was found that
the question would have to be resub-
mitted to the people. This was a great
disappointment. It would involve more
outlay of work and money.

Would George continue his labors?

CHAPTER XII.

UNFULFILLED PROMISES.

Nothing daunted by the late defeat, for his was a sanguine heart, George began early to plan for a new campaign. He surveyed the field, took his bearings and again entered the conflict with all the earnestness of his nature. His individuality was now felt. Whites were inclined to respect his opinions. They said he was a bright man. At the same time he was made to feel that people so long in bondage need not expect much regard from those who enslaved them. He tried to be patient and to overlook slights, but this was difficult to do. Though a decided character, he

was careful to whom he expressed himself. When asked "What will be the
political outcome of all this agitation of
the temperance question?" he modestly
gave his opinion without compromising
his principles, or being offensive. His
keen insight into character led him to
suspect that some to whom he looked
for aid, would likely prove traitors in
the hour of need. During the first
campaign, colored people attended the
same meetings and sat on the same
platform with whites, and were protected
at the voting places; but promises made
then, would have to be fulfilled, before
there would be much co-operation now
on the part of the blacks.

George influenced all with whom he
came in contact not to compromise
with the liquor traffic. He remembered

that the distinguished men who framed
a constitution for the United States,
tolerated slavery, causing great trouble.
If government licenses the liquor traffic,
making it respectable, it should be responsible for the mischief done by men
in drunken brawls.   Though young
at the time George remembered those
stirring events, and that God brought
about the end of slavery and saved the
Union.   He could not forget the bugle's
call and the tramp, tramp of soldiers in
General Sherman's army, as it went
marching toward the sea.   Uncle Ned
came over to their cabin before it was
light, his eyes staring wildly.   As he
came into the cabin he called out,
" Glory, Hallelujah, de Lawd am a
cummin' dis time shuah.   Git down on
yo' knees."   Old and young obeyed,

for he was a preacher and all were taught to respect him It was a characteristic prayer, with but little regard for the rules of syntax; but that earnest prayer of that old man for all de "Ginerals from de Norf what am cum down to set de little and big folkses free; good Lawd, grant dem 'tection by the low ground and victory on the hill top, if it please yer."

The humble prayers that went up from those poor hovels were answered in God's own good time. Their faith was wonderful, and but for it they would have despaired. Surely these poor ones will not again be permitted to be bound down by a worse bondage to their appetites and passions. God forbid that another Abraham Lincoln should have to be raised up to emancipate the millions enslaved to rum.

CHAPTER XIII.

WOMEN HELPERS.

" You remember your dear mother who first stirred the ripple of love in your heart. She is gone; but her influence and lessons survive. That ripple flows on forever.''

The cruel manner in which the colored people were being treated, in many places, was cause of sorrow and anxiety to George.

Word had just come of a cruel lynching in a neighboring State. On account of their repeated acts the freedmen were growing desperate.

One evening George was sitting meditating on these sad events and trying to catch a glimpse of light in the darkness. His arm rested on a table, his

head was bowed and lips moved as if in prayer. '' O, when will my poor despised Afro-American brethren rise above their cruel surroundings? When will the whites treat them as they should be treated? When will the bitter prejudice of those who look upon us as inferior be put away?''

In midst of all there was much to encourage him. As a people they were making as much progress in educational matters as the whites in Georgia.

In one district out of a hundred persons, there was not a half dozen whites who could keep a record of an election. A greater desire for education on the part of whites and blacks was needed as well as more schools.

Only one-fifth of the population could read and write.

In visiting from house to house he had
an opportunity for impressing upon the
women that every lasting reform began
in the homes of the people. Women
were the home-builders. Now that the
fragment of the broken families which
had been scattered, were being gathered
together again, homes could be estab-
lished. A conservative element opposed
women taking part in temperance work;
but a few believed the reform would
not succeed without the help of good
women. While he believed that it was
in the family that woman's most effective
work was done, he did not discourage
those who had time and ability, to aid
in public meetings. He had heard Mrs.
F. E. Harper, a gifted colored woman,
speak on the temperance question. She
had aided in the abolition of slavery and

is now making the sentiment by writing and speaking that will triumph in the abolition of the drink business.

" Will women not neglect their families if they engage in this public work?" asked a conservative.

" Did Mrs. H. B. Stowe neglect her home duties while writing " Uncle Tom's Cabin "? Did Deborah and Miriam, who took part in public affairs, neglect their homes? Did the noble women who braved the dangers of camp life to care for sick and dying soldiers neglect their homes? The grand women who came from the North to teach us, had to leave their homes; but it was because they had the true missionary spirit. They suffered for our sakes, and we cannot be too thankful to them. Some of them are now among the active temperance women of the country; educated, refined women, whose hearts were touched with pity for the ignorant slave. They were missionaries in the truest sense, and deserve to have their names engraved in marble for what they did."

"I glory in woman doing all the good she can, sir; she had much to do in the fall of man; Eve, for instance," said one of George's friends.

"It looks as if men would never forgive women for this first wrong step. They will go on down the ages, twitting women about it, taking advantage of their example," said George with a mischievous look.

"Yes, Adam loved fruit, and Eve's daughters have been tempting men with the wine cup ever since."

"Yes, wicked men are always **ready**

to yield to temptation. They give good women a great deal of trouble, but with their help men will do better the next century. At any rate the women of the twentieth century will be thankful for the pioneer workers on the two great questions. Did not women prepare the way for their sisters now to rise in the scale of intelligence and virtue, making better wives and mothers; better home keepers; more useful women in the world?"

CHAPTER XIV.

USEFUL TRADES AND DOMESTIC SCIENCE.

The fear of the Lord is the beginning of wisdom ; and the knowledge of the holy is understanding.—PROVERBS, 9 : 10.

" Massa George, will de white folks ebber respect us colored folks? "

" It will depend on how well we behave ourselves," said George, thoughtfully. " We must not expect too much at first. We should begin right, live sober, upright lives, and be respectable in our conduct. Our young people should be trained in useful trades and domestic science, and attendance at such schools should be compulsory.

Domestic economy is more important to us than political. It begins in the home. The training and discipline to be had in industrial schools is needed to make us more steady and persevering. We incline too much to change from one kind of work to another. We want no caste education. It is brains, not blood or titles or wealth that make men great and good in this world. Only consistent, Christian character can do that."

All did not possess the brains George had. By his perseverance and hard study, he was becoming a useful man. He taught his people to respect honest labor, and not to look down on the man or woman who is trying to earn a living in any useful employment.

" We should not encourage an aristocracy of blood or money in this repub-

lican land of ours," said George, "we
want to dignify labor and make it respectable.   We must admit that we had
something to do in fostering the idea of
an aristocracy.   It is one of the things
we learned well in slavery which created
an aristocracy.   We looked up to the
white man who had money and slaves.
He had influence.   Our people rather
liked big folks and sometimes quarreled
over the respectability of masters and
mistresses, their riches and blood, and
if there was a colonel or judge connected
with our masters' families, we were
proud to tell it, and took credit to ourselves on account of it.

"Men transmitted their habits to their
children and servants, and this accounts
for so much intemperance and vice
among us to-day.   In this free land,

every man has a chance, if he behave himself, be he a rail-splitter, a tanner or a tailor, if only he is upright, intelligent and honest, and does his work well. It is so much stock in trade."

Here a man came in to tell of another sad lynching.

A white man sold a black man a horse that broke into the white man's pasture and did some damage. The white man told the black man to keep the horse out, but he got into the cornfield a second time and the white man kept the horse. The black man, taking his gun, went and demanded his horse, but the white man refused. The black man came the third time and with profane words demanded his horse. The white man shot him and followed him and shot over his lifeless body. Nothing

was done with him. He was afraid of
a colored woman who had seen him
shoot the black man. When the shoot-
ing was found out, a posse of white men
went to her home, and put a rope
around her neck, drew her up and tried
to force her to tell who the man was.
She begged the mob to let her down. A
man suggested that they give her a
severe whipping, to which all agreed,
and they fell to and beat her, and shot
off guns over her head. She appealed to
the colored people for protection. Word
having spread that she was lynched, a
number of colored men started to hunt
for her body, and when they found her
they took her to town and made complaint to the sheriff. The County At-
torney refused to receive the complaint
from the victim, although she told who

the men were who strung her up to the limb of a tree; that the men might whip her. The officials told her and her protectors that they would lock them up if they did not stop telling lies on nice white men. Every man that came with her was spotted, so the mob could wreak its vengeance upon them. The mob then visited her brother, a school trustee and a hard working farmer, and placed ropes around their necks, and punched them with guns and made them tell the names of every man that went to rescue the girl. After kicking and abusing them some time the leader asked: " Do you —— niggers want to pray?"

" Yes, boss," they replied.

Another of the mob said, " You have had *too* much time to pray already."

" String them up, boys, said the leader." And up they went, without trial or jury, two on one limb. The limb bent and their legs were tied up to their thighs, so their bodies would swing clear of the ground. Their tongues were protruding from their mouths, and their eyes from their sockets. They died by strangulation, and with great suffering. The three lifeless bodies presented a horrible and ghastly sight. Two hundred blacks and whites witnessed this mob. The coroner's jury rendered the usual verdict; "Death by parties to the jury unknown."

The justice knew the names of half the mob who committed the terrible deed, five of whom were present looking at the work they had done; and all the county officers approved of what the mob had done.

CHAPTER XV.

AN ELOQUENT ADDRESS.

" Come all ye men who love the right,
  Keep in de middle ob de road.
  Come aid us in this glorious fight,
  Keep in de middle ob de road.
  We'll hurl the rum-king from the throne,
  Then, God, the Lord, shall have his own,
  And liberty to all make known,
  Keep in de middle ob de road.
  Den children, keep in de middle ob de road,
  Don't you turn to de right, don't turn to de left,
  But keep in de middle ob de road."

The time was near at hand for the final vote on the amendment. A large mass meeting was called, and people turned out in crowds to hear what George, among other speakers, had to say. He never stood before a finer audience, and for over an hour he held his hearers spell-bound. Many were pleased and some were displeased. He spoke in substance as follows :

"Fellow Citizens: Do you want protection to your homes? You now have an opportunity of voting for an amendment to our constitution forever prohibiting the manufacture and sale of liquors in this State. The legislature has submitted the question to the people, who, by their votes, will decide for or against it. The right of self protection is paramount to all others. The supreme court has decided that states have the right to prohibit the traffic in liquors as a menace to our government. It fills the land with pauperism and makes men vicious and insane, ready to commit every foul crime. It imposes heavy taxation on the virtuous and industrious, and unfits men for labor and robs them of their rights as citizens ; destroys the grain God has given man for food and makes poison of it. The private citizen, the legislator, the Judge on his bench, the minister of the Gospel, all fall before the seductive influence of drink. Thousands every year go down to dishonored graves through love of it. This habit is sapping the life's blood of the nation, filling the land with poverty and crime.

"What are you going to do about it, brethren? Vote it out? License, high or low, is not the remedy. It is a compromise with the liquor traffic. In slavery times we had the Missouri Compromise. God did not then, and does not now, approve of any compromise with evil. Constitutional prohibition, with

enforcing statutes, is what Georgia
needs to-day. Will you not rise up in
your might and wipe the liquor traffic
from our State? You can do it by simply
going to the voting places and voting
for the Amendment. It will gladden
the hearts of thousands of wives and
children whose lives are wretched
through this blighting curse. Save the
children, who are the hope of the
country. Years ago you were ready
to lay down your lives in defense of
your homes. My brethren, a greater
danger is at your doors to-day. A terrible foe is robbing wives of husbands,
and children of fathers and mothers and
of heaven itself. Will you not rise in
your manhood, and crush out this
enemy of the home of the rich man
and the working man, and free our

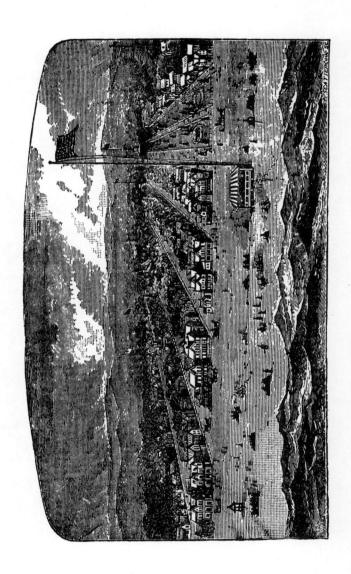

State from the rum power? Suffering humanity demands it; God demands it."

"What are the *parties* going to do with the liquor question?" asked a bright mulatto man.

"Keep on compromising," said George. "I do not profess to be a prophet," said he, rising on tip-toe and looking far away. "It seems to me that if the moral element in all parties will come out and join heart and hand, and work with a new purpose in view—

"Start a new party, sah?" asked a big, burly fellow in the rear of the hall.

"Or reform the old," said the speaker, who proceeded in a solemn tone. "I believe there yet live deep down in the hearts of the people of our Union, principles which, under God, will free us from this worst of slavery, I care not to what party they belong."

There is need of reconstruction in
party platforms.   Would that men generally acknowledged Christ as king and
ruler of our nation.   He hath declared
that all authority "hath been given unto
him in heaven and earth," but men go
on regardless of his law.

"If the Bible were taken as of
supreme authority in the affairs of the
nation, and its precepts followed, there
would be less strife.   When the ideal
party of principle is formed, we shall
see the practical workings of the text,
'God hath made of one blood, all the
nations of men to dwell on all the face
of the earth.'   An ideal party would be
expected to take up living issues that
must be met and settled by thinking
people.

"Brethren, we are part of this nation,

and should take an interest in its having
good laws and in their enforcement.
Other nations are watching this to see
what we will do with these moral questions, the Sabbath, temperance and other
reforms which will be solved in this
country, and we should do our part.
And though government has not always
shown a Christian spirit toward the
black man and the Indian, let us now
show our loyalty by helping to make
our nation a Christian government, as its
founders intended it should be. We,
the people, should do our utmost to
have pure homes, no matter how poor
or plain they are. If civil government
is perpetuated, it will be by each doing
his part to make it pure. " America
holds the future." This nation will solve
all the questions of right and justice,

13

and work out the temperance and labor problems. Let us not complain, my brethren, if we do not enjoy all the privileges that we expected to have when we were set free. The time is coming, if we are prudent, when we shall enjoy all our rights. We hold the balance of power; our ballots will count. Some think giving us the franchise, without requiring some qualifications, was a mistake. A sense of justice compelled the people to give us the ballot, and when it was given to all and not denied to any on "account of race, color or previous condition of servitude," we should be protected in its free use.

The work of reconstruction has not been as satisfactory as we desired, but in time all these matters will be settled in such a way as to be for the good of all concerned. Right will triumph. An

era of peace and prosperity is before us
as a people. We want a chance in life's
battle to live and let live, and to be
trusted with honors when deserving.
Hard though it be to forgive and forget
the past, if we would be forgiven we
should cultivate a forgiving spirit, and
be patient as our Divine leader was
under His trials. "Keep the eye fixed
on Jesus." "As far as possible, let us
live peaceably with all men."

> " Let the thoughts of the cross and the garden,
>   So soften us all with the spirit of heaven,
>   That we may forgive e'en as we are forgiven.''

These plain words addressed to an
audience, including some whites, caused
angry words and threats at the close of
the meeting, and for days after, George
was hounded from place to place, as the
news spread of his speech. Low mur-
murings were heard which could be

traced to the idle, ignorant whites and blacks, who, when under the influence of liquor, imagined they were a much abused people. Politicians were taking advantage of the situation to stir up trouble among them. Every now and again cases of cruelty were reported which added to George's discomfort. A sad case was reported of a woman of position who had a colored mother stripped and tied up by the heels to a tree, four or five feet from the ground. A negro man forced the pump and a negro woman held the hose and drenched her with water, while the cruel woman who employed her stood off and pelted the poor creature with stones and tortured her with a hot iron until she was covered with sores from head to foot.

This inhuman treatment was too much for George, whose kind heart sympathized with his people in all their trials.

CHAPTER XVI.

THREATS.

"Trust your Heavenly Pilot and you will ride out the storm."

The battle waxed hotter and hotter as the day approached for the final vote on the Amendment. Threats of intimidation at the polls were rife, and men were secretly preparing for the conflict. Friends and foes were out early. Men and women and children, in grotesque dress, were out with flags with all manner of inscriptions on them. Men in red shirts on horseback rode recklessly through the crowded streets, uttering terrible oaths in a warlike spirit. The bitter feeling against whites and blacks mingling together at the polling places gave vent to angry threats of vengeance, and many refused to vote with colored people.

In midst of all, in the thickest of the conflict, George was calm and dignified and apparently without a fear.

The cause was right, it was the cause of God and humanity; would not the " God of all the earth do right?" And though at times it looked as if the enemy would triumph, his faith never faltered.

As the day advanced, and men became excited, they came to angry blows, and a man was carried off the ground a lifeless corpse. Many were hurt, and for a time pandemonium reigned.

After the election was over, and men

counted the votes, it was found that the Amendment was lost. Georgia was still under the dominion of King Alcohol.

Soon it was noised about that George was missing. No one remembered seeing him since the fight between two notorious men, Jack Tompkins and Bill Holly. Could it be possible that he had been spirited away? Men were started in every direction and the country was scoured for miles around, if possible to find him. Various stories were started, one that an old hearse was seen driving furiously across the country; another that two men were seen on one horse riding so fast that no one could tell who they were. So great was the excitement that no one could give a straightforward story in regard to it.

What had become of the brave champion of temperance?

CHAPTER XVII.

SCHEME OF WICKED MEN THWARTED.

George had been aware for some time that he had enemies who would not scruple to resort to very low methods to injure his influence; but he did not fear personal violence. His faith was in God, who giveth the victory to the right. He wished every one well, and never dreamed as he went out in the thickest of the fray that morning that wicked men were watching and waiting their opportunity. He happened to be near the two bad men who got into a fight, and while trying to separate them he was picked up and spirited away so rapidly that no one knew where he was taken.

He was thrust into a filthy lock-up, with the lowest and vilest. A mock trial was held, witnesses were brought to convict him of assault with intent to kill. He was sentenced to two years in the mines.

There being no regular penitentiary in Georgia, prisoners were let to men who often made money in the operation. George was let to a company that paid $25,000 a year besides all expenses of keeping, for a large number of prisoners, thus making a large profit to the State.

Being a scholar, he was assigned to a place in the mines where he would be expected to perform the double duty of seeing that all attended to their work,

and of keeping the records of the company. Their plan was carried out in
such a summary manner, that it was
evident it was a scheme of wicked men
to get him out of the way, so as to stop
his work in the temperance cause. They
boasted they would make money out of
the scholar.

The whole proceeding was so devoid
of justice and humanity that it was hard
for George to realize the true situation.
He was sentenced without judge or jury,
to penal servitude, a sort of slavery,
without a chance of saying a word to
clear himself. The cruel act was a one-
sided affair. There was no one to plead
for the prisoner. When George began
to realize what his sentence meant; that
it was nothing less than slavery, he was
indignant, and every feeling of his man-

hood revolted. He determined not to submit without a protest. He sent for the self-constituted officers who had him imprisoned, and requested a hearing. The men swore that he had no right to a hearing; that he was their prisoner; a —— abolition teetotaler. He pleaded most eloquently for them to listen to reason and justice, but they would not. At last he said sadly: "Let me lie down right here and die. I have tried to live as a Christian, to be a man of principle, to do to others as I would have them do to me; but I am still in bondage to my fellow men. My *life* is not my own; my *time* is not my own. I am still a slave to the appetites and passions of wicked men whom I would rescue from drink if they would let me. Has my time come to be mustered out?"

In midst of his pleadings, which fell on hardened ears, he heard loud voices outside. The men inside turned deadly pale and trembled with fear. The door flew open and officers came forward and demanded the prisoner. George turned around, and there stood a venerable looking man, whose eyes filled with tears as he stepped up to George and taking him by the hand, he said: "Is this what you have come to, my good fellow?"

"Yes," said George with a husky voice, "but the cause has gone up. God heard the prayer of the slave, and He heard me now. I am thankful to see you, sir."

He had a suspicion that the gentleman before him was his mother's young massa, for whom he was named. It was even so. She knew of George's trouble, and urged him to have her son released.

"I have been visiting the old home in the South and have heard of your good work. Your mother was almost crazy when she heard of your incarceration." Turning to the men who were there and others who had come to the door, he said, "You laid hands on this free man, one of God's noblémen, who was laboring to save every man of you. You were jealous of his work, and kidnapped and brought him to this horrible prison, and put fetters on the feet that were so willing to run on errands of mercy. You put chains on those hands, that worked night and day for your good. He had it in his heart to save his people from the curse of drink, and not only his people, but the whites, whose example is leading the blacks to ruin. God bless him for what he has already accomplished, and may he long continue in this noble work." Looking earnestly at the guilty men, he said, "I know all about your wicked plot to get this man out of the way of doing good in the world. I have the power to rescue him." He motioned to an officer who stepped up and removed the fetters from his feet, and George walked out a free man.

The guilty men on whom he had kept a watchful eye, were arrested on the spot, and hurried off to stand trial before the proper officers.

As George and his friend turned from the scenes of his late labors, their hearts were filled with gratitude to God for de-

14

liverance from that miserable prison. They acknowledged the hand of a kind Heavenly Father, who rescued him from his enemies, whose first decision was to "string him up," but they afterwards changed it to "work in the mines."

We leave our hero ready equipped for reform work. While North, George had studied these questions. In running a parallel between slavery and the liquor question, he was satisfied that greed of gain and power, as well as appetite, actuated those who introduced and maintained these twin evils. Government began compromising with slavery, and is still doing it with the liquor question. What will the end be? If it was right to give the colored man the ballot when he was freed, is it not right to protect him in his right use of it? Is

it not right to protect him from the in-
toxicating cup?

It was no act of his that brought him
into sinful complicity with this evil, which
is cutting off thousands of loyal colored
men every year. Will government continue as it did in slavery, to wink at
this evil? If government made a mistake in giving the franchise to the colored
people before they were ready for it, it
is not their fault, but having granted it
these poor people should be protected
in their rights.

The colored man is part of this government; he helped to make the country
what it is, and has his inalienable rights
as a citizen. If the South land would
have the blessing of prohibition, it will
have to take voters as they come, whites
and blacks. It is thirty years since they

were liberated, and what have government and societies all done to make the
freedmen more intelligent? Much in
dollars; millions of money it is true, but
all this is but a drop in the ocean compared with the need. Before all these
wards of the nation are taught to read
and write, they must have moral and
financial support. Shall it be given?
Shall George be recognized as a worker
in the reforms of the day; or shall he be
ostracised as unworthy of recognition,
because he was once a slave? Shall
he not have a chance to protect himself
from the ravages of rum? Shall he not
have aid in doing so? We leave the
matter with the reader, hoping that the
golden rule will be applied and the
dominant race will help their down-trodden brethren to become as God intended

they should, honorable, useful citizens of this great country.

George needed quiet, and his friend Dr. W. gave him the means of going North to the famous sea-side resort at Ocean Grove, N. J., to rest a while. Dr. W. had spent a season there, and knew the Christian treatment colored people received.

It happened that George arrived there about the time of the colored folks' jubilee held every season. The kindness shown them and the pleasure enjoyed by all, on that occasion, quite captivated him.

The hospitality and the freedom and safety of their grounds, no liquors being permitted, no Sabbath mails, or desecration of any kind, were to him a most delightful object lesson. He was shown

many marks of respect from the kind
citizens.   Dr. Stokes, President of the
Ocean Grove Association, and Clinton
B. Fiske, the freedmen's friend, invited
him to speak; and when leaving, asked
him to come again.   When he heard
that the blue and the gray had met on
this holy ground, and had shaken hands
over their differences, he thought the
millennium was near.

Bidding farewell to this safe resting
place, where there was nothing to hurt
men, he exclaimed in an ecstacy of delight, FREE AT LAST.